BABY RHYMES

A NEWBORN BLACK & WHITE BOOK

a SEQUEL TO ♡

DIDDLE	ITSY BITSY	TEA POT	TWINKLE
AIKEN DRUM		MUFFIN MAN	
MACDONALD	The B♡by's handb♡ok — With over 20 songs that every kid should know	MULBERRY	
ROCK-A-BY	HICKORY	LITTLE LAMB	PAT-A-CAKE

By DAYNA MARTIN

ENGAGE BOOKS
VANCOUVER

ENGAGE BOOKS

Mailing address
PO BOX 4608
Main Station Terminal
349 West Georgia Street
Vancouver, BC
Canada, V6B 4A1

www.engagebooks.com

Written & compiled by: Dayna Martin
Edited & designed by: A.R. Roumanis
Photos supplied by: Shutterstock

FIRST EDITION / FIRST PRINTING

LIBRARY AND ARCHIVES CANADA CATALOGUING IN PUBLICATION

Title: Baby Rhymes / by Dayna Martin.

Other titles: A Newborn Black & White Book

Names: Martin, Dayna, 1983–, author

Description: Sequel to: The baby's handbook.

Identifiers: Canadiana (print) 20190143614 | Canadiana (ebook) 20190143630
ISBN 978-1-77226-624-5 (hardcover). –
ISBN 978-1-77226-692-4 (softcover). –
ISBN 978-1-77226-625-2 (pdf). –
ISBN 978-1-77226-626-9 (epub). –
ISBN 978-1-77226-627-6 (kindle)

Subjects: LCSH: Nursery rhymes, English.

Classification: LCC PZ8.3.M37 BL 2019 | DDC J398.8 – DC23

 HUMPTY **4**

 EENY MEENY **6**

 JACK & JILL **8**

 BOY BLUE **10**

 **12** PECKLED FROG

 **14** BO-PEEP

 **18** MISS MUFFET

 **20** LITTLE PIGGY

 **22** LONDON BRIDGE

26 HUSH LITTLE BABY

 **28** RUB-A-DUB

 **36** BROTHER JACK

 **38** BUCKLE MY SHOE

40 LITTLE MONKEYS

 **42** MOTHER HUBBARD

 **44** FIVE DUCKS **3**

Humpty Dumpty sat on a wall,
Humpty Dumpty had a great fall.

4

All the king's horses
and all the king's men,
Couldn't put Humpty
together again.

Eeny, meeny, miny, moe,
Catch a tiger by the toe.

If he hollers, let him go,
Eeny, meeny, miny, moe.

Jack and Jill went up the hill
To fetch a pail of water.

Jack fell down and broke his crown,
And Jill came tumbling after.

9

Little Boy Blue,
Come blow your horn,
The sheep's in the meadow,
The cow's in the corn;
But where is the boy
Who looks after the sheep?

He's under a haystack,
He's fast asleep.
Will you wake him?
No, not I,
For if I do,
He's sure to cry.

Five little speckled frogs
Sat on a speckled log
Eating the most delicious
bugs. (yum yum)

12

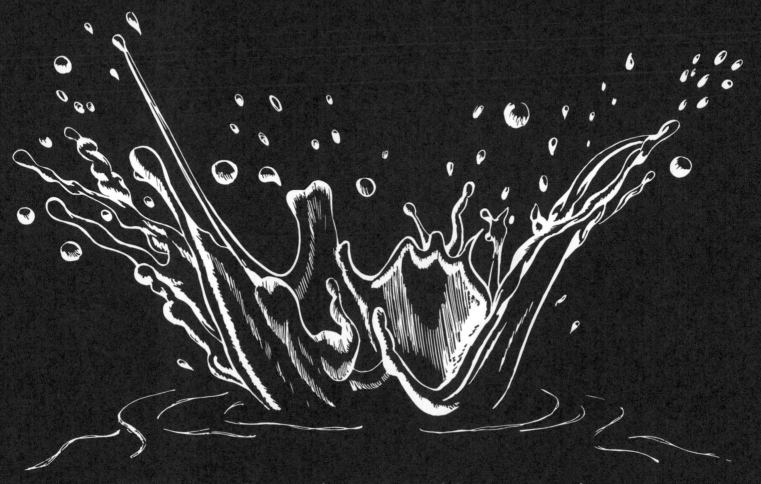

One jumped into the pool
Where it was nice and cool
Then there were four green
speckled frogs. (glub glub)

Repeat until there are no frogs left.

Little Bo-Peep has lost her sheep,
and doesn't know where to find them;

14

Leave them alone,
And they'll come home,
wagging their tails behind them.

It's raining; it's pouring.
The old man is snoring.

He went to bed and bumped his head,
And didn't wake up the next morning.

Little Miss Muffet
Sat on a tuffet,
Eating her curds and whey;

18

Along came a spider
Who sat down beside her
And frightened Miss Muffet away.

19

This little piggy went to market,
This little piggy stayed home,

This little piggy had roast beef,
This little piggy had none,
And this little piggy cried
wee wee wee all the way home.

21

London Bridge is falling down,
Falling down, falling down.

London Bridge is falling down,
My fair lady.

The three little kittens
they lost their mittens,
And they began to cry.
Oh, mother dear, we sadly fear
Our mittens we have lost.

24

What? Lost your mittens,
you naughty kittens!
Then you shall have no pie.
Mee-ow, mee-ow, mee-ow.
We shall have no pie.
Our mittens we have lost.

Hush, little baby, don't say a word,
Mama's going to buy you a mockingbird.
If that mockingbird won't sing,
Mama's going to buy you a diamond ring.

26

If that diamond ring turns brass,
Mama's going to buy you a looking glass.
So hush little baby, don't you cry,
Daddy loves you and so do I.

Rub-a-dub-dub,
Three men in a tub.
And who do you think they were?

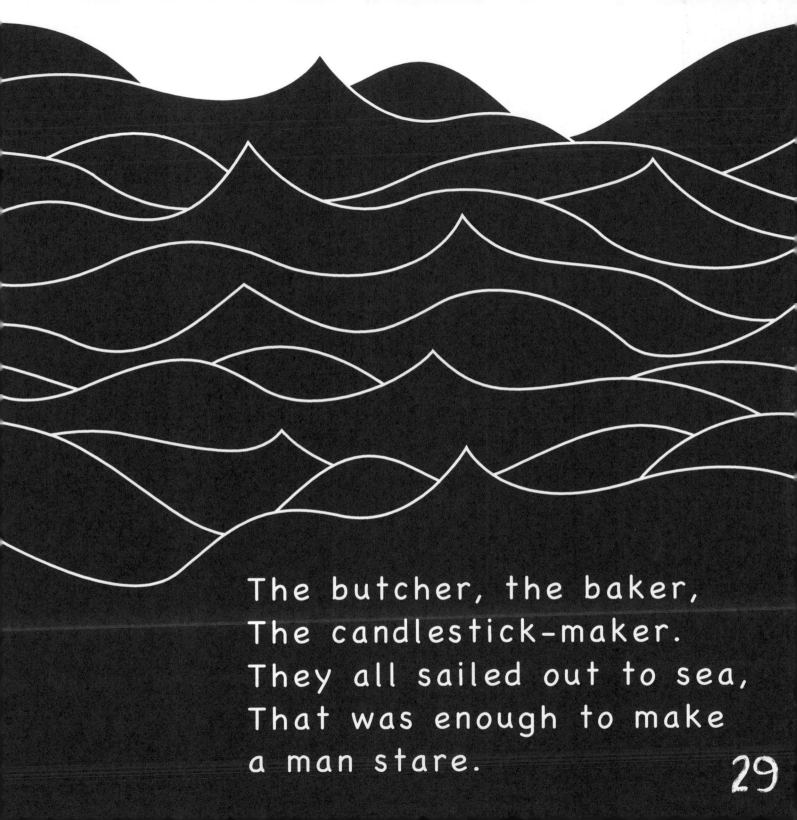

The butcher, the baker,
The candlestick-maker.
They all sailed out to sea,
That was enough to make
a man stare.

29

Sing a song of sixpence,
A pocket full of rye.
Four and twenty blackbirds,
Baked in a pie.

30

When the pie was opened
The birds began to sing;
Wasn't that a dainty dish,
To set before the king.

Peter Piper picked a peck
of pickled peppers.
A peck of pickled peppers
Peter Piper picked.

If Peter Piper picked a peck
of pickled peppers,
Where's the peck of pickled peppers
that Peter Piper picked?

33

Tweedledum and Tweedledee
Agreed to have a battle;
For Tweedledum said Tweedledee
Had spoiled his nice new rattle.

34

Just then flew down a monstrous crow,
As black as a tar-barrel;
Which frightened both the heroes so,
They quite forgot their quarrel. 35

Are you sleeping?
Are you sleeping?
Brother Jack.
Brother Jack.

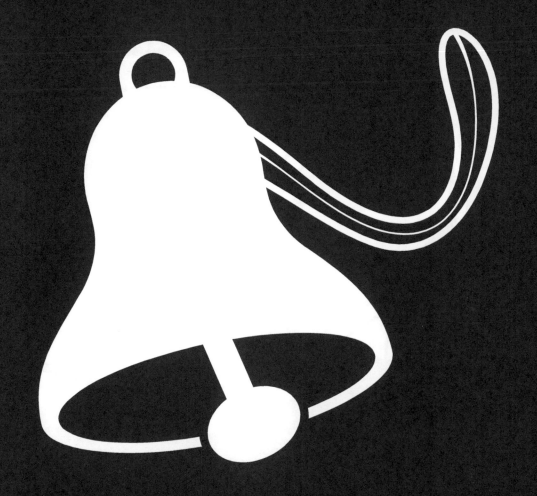

Morning bells are ringing.
Morning bells are ringing.
Ding Ding Dong.
Ding Ding Dong.

37

One, two, buckle my shoe;
Three, four, knock at the door;
Five, six, pick up sticks;
Seven, eight, lay them straight:
Nine, ten, a big fat hen;

Eleven, twelve, dig and delve;
Thirteen, fourteen, maids a-courting;
Fifteen, sixteen, maids in the kitchen;
Seventeen, eighteen, maids in waiting;
Nineteen, twenty, my plate's empty.

Five little monkeys jumping on the bed,
One fell off and bumped his head.

Mama called the doctor and the doctor said:
"No more monkeys jumping on the bed!"

Repeat until you reach one monkey:

Now there's no little monkeys jumping on the bed.

Old Mother Hubbard
Went to the cupboard,
To give the poor dog a bone;

When she came there,
The cupboard was bare,
And so the poor dog had none.

43

Five little ducks went out one day
Over the hill and far away
Mother duck said
"Quack, quack, quack, quack."
But only four little ducks came back.

Repeat until there are no ducks left:

Mother duck went out one day
Over the hill and far away
The sad mother duck said
"Quack, quack, quack."
And all five little ducks came back.

Jack be nimble,
Jack be quick,
Jack jumped over
The candlestick.

Find more early concept books at www.engagebooks.com

About the Author

Dayna Martin is the mother of three young boys. When she finished writing *The Toddler's Handbook* her oldest son was 18 months old, and she had newborn twins. Following the successful launch of her first book, Dayna began work on *The Baby's Handbook*, *The Preschooler's Handbook*, and *The Kindergartener's Handbook*. The ideas in her books were inspired by her search to find better ways to teach her children. The concepts were vetted by numerous educators in different grade levels. Dayna is a stay-at-home mom, and is passionate about teaching her children in innovative ways. Her experiences have inspired her to create resources to help other families. With thousands of copies sold, and translations in twenty different languages, her books have already become a staple learning source for many children around the world.

Translations

ASL (SIGN)	ITALIAN
ARABIC	JAPANESE
DUTCH	KOREAN
ENGLISH	MANDARIN
FILIPINO	POLISH
FRENCH	PORTUGUESE
GERMAN	PUNJABI
GREEK	RUSSIAN
HEBREW	SPANISH
HINDI	VIETNAMESE

Have comments or suggestions?
Contact us at: alexis@engagebooks.ca

Show us how you enjoy your **#handbook**. Tweet a picture to **@engagebooks** for a chance to win free prizes.